Cosy Burrow Books

VALKYRIE ACADEMY DRAGON ALLIANCE
Book Six

AMBUSHED

I0593074

"Against all odds, Valkyries winged and wingless must combine forces to save the realm of Asgard in this action-packed tale brimming with magic, mayhem, and a monstrous battle." Angela M., Line Editor, Red Adept Editing

Valkyrie Academy Dragon Alliance Books

Cosy Burrow Books

VALKYRIE ACADEMY DRAGON ALLIANCE

AMBUSHED

KATRINA COPE

ISBN: 978-0-6486613-5-1

Michael ~ your support means the world to me

GET UPDATES & NOTIFICATIONS OF GIVEAWAYS

Would you like a FREE copy of Marked?
Visit here:
https://www.katrinacopebooks.com/valkyrie-academy-dragon-alliance

Through this link you can sign up for my newsletter and receive a FREE copy of Marked plus updates about my fantasy books, sales and notification of giveaways.

- CHAPTER ONE -

Rocks crumble from the ceiling and wall,

clattering around me, filling the cave. I crumple
to my knees, close my eyes, and hold up my
hands, willing protection for my head. The
clattering rocks continue to fall around me, yet
none hit my flesh. Daring myself to look, I
slowly pry open one eye to observe the chaos.
A massive gush of breath expels from my
lungs. Purely by fluke, I have created a barrier,

protecting me from the stones. It's perfect timing for another gift to manifest.

I glance around the room, watching the destruction pile around me. *What have I done?* I should grab Gilroma, run for the cave door, and exit this mountain before it collapses on top of us.

Frantically, I search for the dark elf. I find him hunkered down in the back corner, arms raised to shield himself from the rocks toppling around him. Even though we can protect our tiny little spot with our magic, it is not going to save us from the whole mountain collapsing on top of us. We will become trapped within the mountain and buried alive.

The prickling sensation of my magic leaves my left arm and circulates through my whole body. It was this sensation of the magic and the power that travels with it that caused this destruction. Under Gilroma's instruction, I was merely practicing my magic within the small cave and got too excited, so I used too much of it. This always leads to catastrophe, as I've yet to finesse my control over it.

I glance at the pile of magic books and wonder if I should grab a handful and make a dart for the exit. These books are priceless. I bound forward, reach the books, then turn to see what Gilroma is doing. I nearly drop the books. The dark elf has risen to his feet and is spreading his arms wider, his protection expanding with his motion. The rocks fall farther away from him as they continue to crumble off the mountain. He swings his arms wildly then pushes his hands toward the ceiling. The rumbling and rattling stop, and the rain of rock ceases. I ogle as the larger rocks that have fallen to the floor rise into the air and secure themselves into their original position.

My jaw drops, and I stare at him in amazement. "You can do that?"

His glowing yellow eyes stare at me. "Of course. It is not the first time this little cave suffered a major catastrophe. Besides, this is the way the cave was made in the first place. Do you really think a cave attached to such a long tunnel burrowing deep into a mountain is natural?"

"I hadn't thought about it. It's not exactly a kind of place I would normally hang around. You are the first being I've known who lives in the middle of a mountain."

"This little cave was made by me. This is my safe little secure hidey-hole. So I can reverse any damage that comes to it."

The final stone shifts into place, and we breathe out a large combined breath and stand straight. I replace the books on the pile then look at my palms, tossing my sight from one palm to the other. I'm still amazed that I hold such great power and my hands caused so much damage. The zmey marked me again today, striking me down my torso, and it seems to have accentuated my magic. I no longer hold this magic only within my left arm. With Gilroma's help, it runs through both arms, and now it has been released through my entire body thanks to the zmey scratching my torso.

Gilroma stands tall, his glowing eyes burning stronger as he looks at me. "You need to learn how to control your power. Sometimes, a slower release is more powerful than an instant burst of magic." His voice is gritty and deep.

"I'm sorry. I understand. I will try." I wipe away beads of sweat that accumulated while I tried to save myself from being buried alive.

"All right. I want you to concentrate on the magic soaring through your body."

I do as he asks and let the magic well inside my torso, feeling its power extending to my limbs.

"I want you to let it sit and swell. Feel it. Breathe it as it flows through your body. You need to become one with this magic. That way, you can execute any power or defense that runs through your mind."

I close my eyes and picture this in my head until I feel at one with the magic swirling through my body. I nod as an indication that I have completed this process.

"Now, bring it to rest in your fingers and hold your hands in a cup, bringing them close together. Feel the magic toss between your fingers as you spread them wide."

I can feel the magic precisely as he describes. It is a strange feeling, having it swirl across my fingertips in a constant movement yet still attached to my body. For a simple wingless Valkyrie like me, it is surreal to have this power. But I'm grateful that the creature chose me, for whatever reason. Surely, this has to prove that I'm better than the winged Valkyries give me credit for.

"Now focus. Focus on that prickling sensation and the well you can feel on your fingertips. Hang on to it. Don't let it escape. Let it build on disappointments and betrayals from the past. Learn to use those emotions to your advantage."

As I sit and let the magic well within my fingertips, I recall how the dark elf had told me that Odin is the reason the winged Valkyries have their reaping powers. The wingless don't have it, purely because Odin chose not to give it to them. He has the ability to provide the gift to wingless Valkyries but refuses.

The power whirls within my fingertips, and anger churns deep inside. To think that we have been pushed aside, all because we were born without wings, spirals my rage out of control. A spurt of magic bursts forth, blasting into the wall and dislodging many of the replaced rocks from the ceiling and walls.

I throw my hands up, shielding myself from the falling rocks that are destroying the cave. "Whoops. That didn't go so well."

"You didn't contain your power again like I instructed you to." Gilroma's hairless eyebrows drop in a scowl. "You're supposed to hold onto that and release it slowly, with control, not blast it into the wall." He holds his hands above his head, controlling his magic, then swings his arms around and pushes his hands toward the ceiling. The rocks return to their original positions. Despite this being the second time I have seen him do this, this feat is quite fascinating, and I can't help staring in wonder at the returned rocks. I hope I can do this one day too.

"I know. I'm sorry. I was distracted by what you told me about Odin. And I guess my anger intensifies when mixed with my magic."

"You need to execute control over this, even when your anger surfaces. An angry fighter is a losing fighter. They are too overpowered by anger to see reason and judge the situation correctly."

I grit my teeth. "I know. I'm sorry. I need to learn how to control this better." I'm surprised the dark elf isn't yelling at me by now. If this were Odin or Mistress Sigrun, I would have been drilled ages ago, not that the yelling succeeded in training me quicker. I admire the elf's patience. It encourages me to work harder to please him.

After he fixes the cave, I work on drawing my magic, letting it swirl and controlling it properly. Slowly, I aim it toward the wall and start to draw out the loose rocks one by one, focusing on one section and digging a small hole into the side of the mountain. Several rocks clink to the ground, and a crescendo of clattering sounds fills the room, but this time, there's no reason to panic. The magic is well controlled, and I'm executing the command slowly and steadily, eliminating the fear of the cave falling on top of us. I continue to work on the hole with my magic, pulling out all the loose rocks and slowly piling them along the side of the tunnel. Maintaining my composure, I let the magic continue its work until another small room has formed next to the room that we're in, adding an extension to the tiny cave.

"Good. Very good. You have learned to hold your control over your magic powers. If you keep practicing, you will be able to use magic efficiently against your opponent." Gilroma's yellow eyes gleam with pride as he looks at me. "After some more practice, you will manifest control whether you execute your power rapidly or slowly."

"So does this mean that I can direct it at Odin and rip out small clumps of hair, especially from his beard, bit by bit until he gives me the power to reap souls?"

The dark elf looks at me wide-eyed for a moment then chuckles. "With an attitude like that, you would fit in nicely with the dark elves. That's a rather sadistic way of trying to obtain something. It's almost a shame that you are joking. You know guys are weaklings when it comes to hair removal, don't you?"

"Oh, I know. It's a perfect form of torture." I grin widely. "Then he should give me what I want."

- CHAPTER TWO -

Feeling empowered, I exit the cave and follow the narrow tunnel. Aided by my magic, the rocks hover around me and clatter against the narrow passageway as they follow me out of the mountainside. When the sun warms my face, with a flick of a hand, I dump the rocks unceremoniously in a pile outside the cave.

The magic continues to course through my veins, and now that I am familiar with the feeling, I welcome its power. If I can almost make a mountaintop crumble on top of me, what else can I achieve after more training?

The dark elf has agreed to see me daily and work on crafting my magic. Despite him being such a strange man, I look forward to my next visit.

I climb up the rocky hillside, searching for the spot where I left my saddle and cloak. I half buried them in my rush to see Gilroma, and they are too precious to leave lying around outside.

A strong wind blows, and a strange shiver runs down my spine. At first, I think the shiver is from the chill in the air, but it's not that cold. Standing straight, I breathe the air in deeply. Something is tainting the air, and it's not a strange smell—it is more of a feeling. I quickly scan the area and come up empty. I haven't had this feeling before. I shrug. Maybe it is a figment of my imagination, making me believe that there is magic in the air in Asgard. Perhaps my developing magic is opening my senses, and something magical is always floating through the air. Maybe it is my magic that I am sensing. I close my eyes and take another deep breath as another gust of wind pushes past. I swear that I can sense something, then I shake my head. It's got to be my imagination and my heightened magic ability.

This new sense is raw and fresh in my veins, stirring up all sorts of feelings. I go back to the place where I buried the saddle and my cape, pull the rocks away, and pick up my belongings before draping them over my arm. I hope that Elan is lying invisible and resting. I still don't trust Odin and his men. Despite him saying that he will not capture Elan or harm me, I have not seen any proof that Odin will keep his word.

A dark shadow passes over me, and I gaze up. A dragon circles above, his arms spread wide with membranous wings attached to them. The dragon tilts slightly, giving me a clear view of the many spiky horns covering its head. When the sun glistens off its scales, I catch a glimpse of brown. It's Drogon. He is the dragon who most closely resembles a bat. Flapping hard a few times, he rises into the air then suddenly dives. A scream erupts from above.

Squinting, I spot Hildr's legs hooked around Drogon's neck, and as he twirls in the sky, one of Hildr's hands clasps firmly on one of Drogon's horns while she holds the other high like she is enjoying the joyride. When they swoop past me, I catch a glimpse of her face, and it beams. She releases more screams filled with delight.

I smile. Although I have ridden Elan many times, the magnificence of the ride still takes my breath away. It is a wonderful feeling, and flying on top of the dragon relieves the soul.

A second figure follows Drogon with wings outspread and dots like stars lining his medium-blue wings. Legs are hooked around

Naga's neck as he turns and executes several different maneuvers. Naga dives, and Eir is clasping his neck. A broad smile spreads across her face.

Naga lowers his flat head and stares at me. His blue eyes are wide and full of delight. The sound of beating wings fills the air as he circles around another time then lowers to the ground before landing with a soft thud. Eir climbs off his back. Her smile is contagious.

"Oh, I wish I had done this sooner. It's delightful!" Eir staggers my way, still searching for her ground legs. "We'll have to involve more Valkyries and get them riding more dragons. Now I know what it is like to be able to fly like the winged Valkyries. I am convinced the feeling should be spread among all the wingless."

"That's a wonderful idea, Eir. But we don't have any more friendly dragons. And Eingana says she isn't going to give us any more dragons. We can only work with what is already here in the academy. And most of these are too vicious from being mistreated by the winged Valkyries."

"Maybe we can work on the dragons." Eir shakes out her legs as if trying to release the muscles. She is always the peacemaker and willing to see the best in everyone and everything. "I understand they'd be upset from being mistreated, but surely we can work with them and show that the wingless Valkyries are much nicer than the winged. Maybe if they see us working closely with some of the friendly dragons, it will make them want to be on our side."

"It might work. But to make it work, we also have to find a Valkyrie who is strong-willed and determined to ride a dragon. A Valkyrie who would be more likely to work with a dragon that is a bit touchy around Valkyries." I watch Hildr as she flies around on Drogon, crying "Yahoo!" at the top of her voice. "They would have to be a lot like Hildr but perhaps with more patience, especially if the dragon turns out to be like Naga."

Eir grins widely while watching Hildr. "I'm glad Hildr was too impatient for Naga. Her loss is my gain. Besides, she seems to have found her perfect match, and Drogon didn't make it easy for her." She looks at Hildr for a while longer. "What about Britta? She seems like she has a strong will."

I rub my thumb across my chin. "You know, I think you're right. She did seem to be quite strong-willed. And she said she supported our cause and was happy to see that others were willing to oppose the winged Valkyries."

Another puff of cool breeze brushes past me, and I frown. Something definitely seems to be traveling on the breeze. "Did you feel that?"

Eir looks at me with disbelief. "Feel what?"

"I don't know. There seems to be something on the air. Something strange."

"Like what? I didn't feel anything."

I shrug. "I'm not sure. It could be just me. Not long ago, the zmey chased me down and scratched my torso."

Eir's eyes widen, and I continue. "Apparently, it was marking me with more magic, and ever since then, magic has been manifesting strongly and coursing through my body."

Eir clasps her hands together. "That's exciting. What can you do?"

"I'm still working on it. I think I can do something with that rock." I point at a rock not far away. "Just give me a minute." I hold my hands as if grasping an imaginary bowl, and I pull at the magic within my body, allowing it to well as the dark elf taught me. When it feels right, I let the magic fly into the boulder. The magic hits the rock, and it explodes like it's been hit by a bomb.

Eir gasps, and Naga stares at the rock. *That's impressive*, he says telepathically. *Naga not seen that from people before.*

"I think that's a good thing, that you haven't seen magic from Valkyries before, Naga. If the winged Valkyries held this magic, they might have used it against the dragons. I don't know why the creature keeps marking me, but I'm going to use this gift for the right reasons. I'm going to prove that I'm worth as much as these winged Valkyries."

Kara don't need to prove to Naga. Kara is good —and Eir and Hildr. All three is better than winged Valkyries, he says in his broken English. I walk forward and stroke his forehead, and he leans into my hand. He's so cute, with such an adorable personality, and he is full of kindness.

"You are an extraordinary dragon. You have such a big heart. Don't lose it."

A loud thump sounds behind me. I spin around to find Drogon has landed on the ground, and Hildr is climbing off his back.

"What was that?" she calls, looking frantic and staring at the pile of shattered rocks.

19

"Kara was just showing me some of the new magic she received from that zmey this morning." Eir stands next to me, placing a hand on my shoulder.

Hildr stares at me. "What do you mean?"

"The zmey marked me again, and my magic has increased. So I've been working on channeling it so I know how to use it properly. One thing I've learned I can do is explode rock, which is what I showed Eir."

"I wish it would mark me." Hildr's pale lip protrudes in a pout.

"I have no idea why it marked me. It does hurt. There is no magic without pain, that's for sure."

Drogon's brown eyes fix on me, and he looks intimidating. His horn-covered head resembles a porcupine lacking several spikes. He has a fierce look that often matches his temperament, but his eyes give him away—he is a big softie underneath.

"Drogon, do you know any dragons that might want to be hooked up with another Valkyrie?" I ask.

His brow creases, and a couple of his horns push together, almost giving him the appearance of a brown unicorn. *There might be one. But they might be a fair bit more aggressive than what I was.*

"What are you thinking?" Hildr asks.

"We think maybe we should bring Britta in and join her with another dragon," I say. "If we can't go to Midgard and reap souls, then perhaps we can learn how to build an army here and fight against any threat that comes to Asgard."

Hildr frowns. "What do you mean we can't reap souls? Didn't you just go to Midgard to help out the winged Valkyries because you earned the right?"

"Yeah, I did go to Midgard, but I couldn't reap souls. Apparently, the wingless haven't been gifted with the gift at all. Odin purposely skips us when he decides to give out the powers. Or that's what I've been told. In any case, I tried to reap souls, and it didn't work. I made a fool of myself again, trying to help out. If it weren't for Harut, then I would feel like an idiot."

"Who's Harut?" Hildr asks.

"Oh, he's just a good-looking angel of death."

"What?" Eir flings her hands by her side. "You haven't mentioned him before."

"You're friends with our enemy?" Hildr asks.

"Yes. And it is complicated. The angels of death are our enemies, but Harut stood up for me ever since the first day I crashed Midgard. For some reason, he decided to take me under his wing because I didn't have wings—"

"Oh, I see what you did there." Hildr slaps her hand against her thigh. "Nice pun."

I roll my eyes. "I didn't mean it like that." I shake my head. "Because I was different from the winged Valkyries, he looked after me. He's never seen a wingless one before. He's been kind ever since my first trip, and I ran into him this trip. And again, he helped me."

"And yes, he is good-looking?" Eir's eyes twinkle.

"Yes, Eir. What's your point?" Despite my gruff words, I feel the heat rising around my ears and flushing to my neck. I try to pretend it isn't there.

"Nothing." She pretends to look innocent. "I was merely wondering if you're going to be the first one to have a little Valkyrie."

That does it. I can feel the blood rush faster to my face, and there's no hiding it. Hildr and Eir both keel over with laughter.

In an attempt to divert attention from me, I accumulate my magic, letting it stir in a combined mass. I focus on a pile of dirt and use my power to lift the mass up and throw it at the back of their heads. Dirt scatters all over their hair and down their shoulders. The laughing stops.

"Oh, Kara!" Eir exclaims, shaking out her leather top, her nose screwing up in disgust.

"We were just having some fun with you." Hildr dusts off her clothes with harsh strokes.

Observing their bewildered faces, I laugh. Suddenly, I'm overcome with exhaustion, my head twirls with dizziness, and I crumple to the ground. My vision distorts, and I see blurry images of Hildr and Eir darting for me before everything turns black.

- CHAPTER THREE -

Something wet and cold drapes across my
face and eyes then wipes across my forehead,
pulling my mind from the depths of darkness.
It takes an effort to pry my eyes open enough
to peer through the cracks. Eventually, my
vision focuses, and I take in the worried look
on Anita's face. I gaze around the room, slowly
taking in the details. We are alone in the
healer's quarters, and I am lying on one of the

few gurneys. The crisp white sheets beneath me rustle as she lifts the head end of my cot. I focus on Anita. The worry hasn't left her face.

"There you are." A sad smile spreads across her face and ripples to her eyes. "I was wondering where you were. You've been gone for days."

I stare at her in confusion. "What do you mean?" My voice is raspy from lack of use.

"Exactly as I said. You've been unconscious for days."

Using my elbow, I prop myself up into a sitting position. "How?"

"Hildr and Eir said you had just used your magic to throw some dirt over them." She gives me a strange look. "Then you collapsed not long afterward. Does this ring any bells?"

I gaze down at my body and see my torn, dirty leathers are gone. I am clean and dressed in my pajamas. Someone has taken care of me while I've been passed out. A surge of worry shoots through my body when I remember my saddle and cloak. I take another look around the room and spot them in the far left corner, sitting on a visitor's lounge chair. I expel a sigh of relief. I know that these are only possessions, but I spent a lot of time making them, and they hold a special place in my heart, connecting me to Elan. I look at the healer. "I remember a little bit. They were teasing me about something, and I used my magic on them."

A knowing look crosses her face, and something briefly dances in her eyes. "Did you do something different? Do you always feel dizzy like that? Have you ever passed out after using magic?"

I shake my head. "I don't feel dizzy using the magic. It's possibly because I was using it too much. I spent a lot of time with Gilroma, the dark elf that you directed me to, and we practiced using it for quite a long time before I ran into Hildr and Eir. The dizziness showed up out of nowhere and overcame me. I must've overexerted myself."

Anita places the washer on the marble bench next to my gurney. A curly auburn lock falls across her eyes, and she hooks it behind her ear. "I hear magic can do that. If you're not used to wielding its power, it can exhaust you quickly. You will have to be careful."

I lean my head back against the firmness of the mattress, and she washes my brow some more. The coolness is a welcome relief for my forehead.

"How did you get to know Gilroma? He's an unusual character for a Valkyrie to be associated with."

She smiles wanly. "Aren't you associated with him right now?"

"Well, yes. But you directed me to him." I frown at her unusual comment.

"Believe it or not, I, too, needed his help at one stage. I was in search of the healer that nobody could give me. I had tried to be brave and fight alongside the winged Valkyries, but I was struck down in an attack on Asgard. The winged Valkyries left me for dead out in the open. It was the elf who stumbled across me and started to heal me. This is why, despite him being an unusual character, I trust him and directed you to him." She replaces the washer on the bench. "I asked him one day why he helped me, and he said that it was merely because he could see the value within me." Her eyes are sad as she recalls the memory. "Even though the Valkyries left me to die and thought I was nothing because I am wingless, he believed I was a value to Asgard." She looks at me with a sincere expression. "If he didn't see value in you, then he wouldn't have helped you either. But I knew there is a value in you that was neglected by the winged Valkyries, which is why I sent you to him. Plus there is the fact that I trust him completely."

"He is a little strange, but he's starting to grow on me. I can't say that he has great people skills." I chuckle. "He's a little rough around the edges."

She laughs with me. "Yes, he is." Her expression turns serious. "You need to make him teach you how to contain that magic so it won't wear you out. I don't know anyone else who can teach this. I am a teacher of healing. I only know how to heal people and teach that, but of magic, I do not know. I do not know how to heal injuries caused by magic, ones that need more than just rest and recuperation."

A ruckus sounds near the entryway of the room.

"Oh, thank Vanir! Look who's finally awake!" Hildr's freckled face comes into my vision.

I smile. I would welcome that spiky hair and that left ear full of earrings any day. Despite her rough exterior, she's a loyal friend. "It's good to see your scruffy face." In reality, she's quite a beautiful redhead. Her coloring is unique compared to that of the rest of the Valkyries, and she has a temper to match her hair.

Next to Hildr, Eir's peaceful face appears wearing a friendly smile. "You're awake! Welcome to the land of the living."

"Yeah, that'll stop you throwing dirt over us next time." Hildr dramatically crosses her arms across her chest. "How rude! Can't handle a little bit of teasing, so you throw dirt over us." She smirks, and the freckles on her cheeks spread.

It takes all my effort to grin. "Yeah, next time I should mix it with water, turning it into a nice muddy mixture. That would go well all over your hair."

She reaches forward, roughing my hair, and my long black strands get caught between her fingers. She yanks my hair.

"Ouch!" I grab her hand and pull it out slowly.

Heavy footsteps enter the doorway. "What's all the ruckus in here?"

I'd recognize that voice anywhere. I glance at the doorway, and Mistress Sigrun has entered the room. Her pale blond hair falls to her shoulders in wavy strands, and her steely blue eyes stare directly at me. "About time you got up, wingless. You've been lounging around way too long. You have chores to do."

Anita stands to face the mistress, placing her hand on her hips. "Mistress Sigrun, she has been unconscious, and she needs her rest."

The mistress glares at her. "I don't care." She lifts her chin and screws her nose in distaste. "She's wingless, just like you. She needs to get up. She has chores to do. End of story!" She spins on her heels and stomps down the corridor.

Anita turns and looks at me. "Stay in bed if you need to. You've been through a lot, and it may take a while for your energy to return."

I slowly push myself onto my elbows. "I've been in here for days. I should get up. I can't have the mistress thinking any less of us."

"I don't think that's possible." Anita shakes her head. "Nothing we do seems to satisfy her."

"I still have chores to finish, anyway. She gave them to me a while ago. I've just been too distracted with working out this magic and fighting winged Valkyries."

"No, you don't. Hildr and I finished them for you." Eir helps to steady me.

I gawk at her in disbelief. "Why would you do that?"

"Because you're our friend." She drags out her words with a playful, condescending tone while giving me a disbelieving glance.

"Then that makes you friends to keep around." I smirk at her.

She huffs with obvious disgust. "Aww. Such dedication!" Eir's voice is tainted with sarcasm.

"You know I don't mean it." I suddenly feel guilty.

"If you do, then you can find the next dragon for a wingless Valkyrie to ride. Tell you what, sticking your head into those stalls is almost as dangerous as flying headfirst into a sword," Hildr says. "But I think we found one."

"Found one for who?" I ask.

"For Britta." Eir rolls her eyes. "Don't you remember?"

The conversation we had before I passed out springs to mind. "Does Britta know about this?"

"Oh yes, she sure does." Hildr nods eagerly. "And she is keen."

Eir holds out a hand to me. "Come on. Let me help you up. I can see you're still weak, but if you're determined to get up, then let me give you a hand."

I clasp her hand and use it to pull myself up. After swinging my feet over the edge of the gurney, I lower them to the floor, and the bed squeaks as I stand slowly.

Hildr slaps my black leather fighting uniform on the bed. "Get these on, and then we can eat. It's lunchtime, and I'm famished. And besides, you need your strength because we have fight class coming up."

- CHAPTER FOUR -

A bout of dizziness overcomes me when I shove back my chair to leave the dining hall, but I push the feeling aside. The majority of my strength has returned after a good meal. Hildr and Eir accompany me to our room, and we retrieve my quiver and bow, my sword, and my sling, which I hook on my back pocket. Once we are all weaponed up, we leave the room and head outside.

"Where are we going?" I ask as we leave the walls of the academy. "Our lessons usually take place inside."

"I know. For some reason, Mistress Sigrun has dragged us outside this time. She notified us just before you woke up."

"And she wanted you to bring me?" I lift an eyebrow. "I thought she wanted me to do chores."

Hildr tosses a dismissive hand at me. "That was just for show. She knows Eir and I completed your chores. It was just another one of her bullying tactics. We're to meet her between the academy and the dragon stalls."

"And we have to hurry." Eir's voice is strained. "We're running late."

"Pfft." Hildr throws her head back. "Don't stress, Eir. We will get there when we get there. Kara had to eat first. She needs her strength."

"I know that. But you know what Mistress Sigrun is like." Eir hooks her long, wavy, light-brown hair into a ponytail while peering at Hildr over her shoulder.

I roll my eyes. "Yeah, I know what she's like. I used to care about what she thought about me, but now her attitude has become quite tiresome. Her threats no longer carry weight like they used to."

A roar rings out from over the hills, and a shiver runs down my spine. It sounds like a dragon roar, one filled with pain. I wonder if Elan heard it and if she's coming to check it out. I know it certainly captured my interest. I hurry my footsteps while yanking my sword from its sheath on my back and clasping it firmly in my right hand. I'm determined to see what is roaring in pain, but I'm not taking any chances. Perhaps it is a dragon that has escaped and is attacking Valkyries.

The ring of two other swords being pulled from their sheaths sounds on either side of me, and in my peripheral vision, I see my two friends flanking my sides as we round the corner of the mountain. I halt at the scene that plays in front of us.

Red glaring eyes stare down at a circle of Valkyries from the red dragon that stands in defensive mode with its back leg chained to a mountain behind it. This chain is long, but the dragon can't escape. A line of white fur travels along the dragon's spine, and at the end of its long, thin tail is a tuft of white fluff. This matches a white fluffy line along her jaw. A camel-like hump forms along her spine, and a long thin neck protrudes from her body.

It is a perfect specimen of the red breed of dragon, which would be more at home decorating a shelf than facing opponents and looking mean and nasty. Flashes of Ness fighting Elan in the wastelands flare through my head. This dragon looks very similar to Ness. It makes me wonder if she is Ness's daughter, who was sacrificed from the red dragon's breed to the Valkyries to honor the alliance between the Valkyries and the dragons.

"Is that Ness's daughter?" I ask.

Both of my friends look at me strangely. "Who's Ness?" Eir asks.

I realize my mistake. I was at the wastelands by myself with only Elan and her family for company. Hildr and Eir wouldn't know Ness. "Ness is a dragon that attacked Elan."

"Lovely!" Hildr's jaw drops.

"She wasn't that bad. Well, she was, but I understand. She hated Valkyries because she knew what they were doing to her daughter. And also because the dragons have to give up a youngling out of their clans every year."

My mind swirls involuntarily at the memory of Ness and her fight against Elan. "Ness injured Elan because Elan was fighting to protect me when I was in the wastelands."

Eir gasps. "That's terrible."

I observe the Valkyries attacking the dragon. The brutality slaps me across the face. Cruel and large gashes run down the front of the dragon. Although the blood blends well with her red scales, there is a slightly darker stream of red that covers several patches of her body where the blood runs from her wounds. "Yeah, at the time, it was terrible that Ness attacked Elan while trying to get me. But as I watch this, I don't blame her. I would be vicious and attack anyone stopping me if my young one was treated like this. And because of her fight, Eingana is making Ness give up one of her babies from every clutch that she lays until further notice. Her babies are to replace the other dragons in her tribe, all because she defied Elan, the second ruler of the dragons. Because she defied Elan, she is seen as having defied Eingana."

"That's atrocious!" Eir hisses. "Oh, Vanir! That's horrible!" She fans her flushed face then slides closer to me and watches the red dragon being attacked again by the Valkyries. "This has to stop. That dragon is still young. Perhaps you have a chance of training her to like us instead of hating us."

"I don't know, Eir." Hildr shakes her head. "I know I wouldn't be too forgiving if I got treated like that."

"Me neither." I agree with Hildr.

It breaks my heart as we watch the Valkyries attack again and again with a mix of weapons, including spears and swords. Mistress Sigrun works in the middle of them, barking out instructions and never holding back when she has a moment to strike the dragon. I remember Sobek's conversation about how spears can go under the scales and pierce the skin into the soft area. Swords dragged over the surface are less likely to cut through, but spears and arrows aimed in the opposite direction of the scales can slide their little tips underneath them. I wince when a spear is thrown at the dragon and torpedoes into her side. A loud bellow from the dragon bursts across the air, turning my stomach into a churning mess.

"I know this is tradition, and the Valkyries use this to train them to fight against dragons, but this is barbaric." Eir's face screws up as if she's in pain. "They must be stopped."

"What I want to know is why Mistress Sigrun says that we are here to practice our fighting skills." A suspicious thought sickens me. "We are the only wingless Valkyries here. All of these others are winged, and we don't fight against dragons. Are you sure you got your information correct?" I turn to Hildr.

Her face, too, appears screwed up with pain as she tugs at her earring-clad ear. "Unfortunately, I'm sure she sent us out here. I have never seen them do this before, and I had no idea where the spot would be. Now I wish I didn't know where the spot was where they ganged up on a single dragon. This is going to give me nightmares every time I pass through this area to go visit Drogon."

I can't help wondering about Elan. Is she flying around the area in her invisible form? If she does know what is going on, is she staying back because it is part of the agreement? It must tear her up inside. Or maybe she doesn't know, and if she found out, she would step in. At least that's what I think she would do.

"I don't know why Mistress Sigrun called us to this area," Hildr says. "I know this is tradition and all, but I can't watch this. The winged Valkyries should learn how to fight without using the live dragon."

We close the distance between the winged Valkyries and the dragon, our feet crunching on the rocks as we step forward. My foot knocks a rock, and it clatters across the ground and lands right in the middle of the fight between the Valkyries and the dragon. Mistress Sigrun pauses and turns around, her eyes an icy-blue color.

"Finally, you have turned up. You're late!" Her eyes narrow as they land on me.

"Are we, Mistress? Why are we here?" I ask.

"Because you need to learn what a dragon should be used for." Her words are spiteful. "Grab a spear and join us," she demands.

- CHAPTER FIVE -

I stare at Mistress Sigrun in disbelief. "Is she serious?" I say loudly enough for Hildr and Eir to hear me.

"Ah, I believe so." Eir's voice is high-pitched.

"Ludicrous!" Hildr spits, her voice slightly louder than ours but, judging by the mistress's face, still not carrying to Mistress Sigrun.

I huff out a laugh. "Eir and I think so."

"I don't think so," Mistress Sigrun says. I cringe. She did hear us. "You want to be part of the winged Valkyries, then this is part of the initiation. You want to fight with us, then you have to learn to fight a dragon." Her voice turns passionate as she says, "You have to learn to fight the dragon, cause it pain, and make it roar." She throws her fist in the air. Then she opens her hand and flips it, flicking it topside first toward the ground. "You have to learn how to bring it down, slicing open its sides and getting through the scales."

My blood boils, and I square my shoulders when I hear five thuds behind us. I peer over my shoulder, and several winged Valkyries are blocking our way back to the academy. They must think we're going to run, but I have a different plan in mind. "Come on, guys," I say as I move forward.

"What? No." Eir sounds panicked.

I grit my teeth and peer over my shoulder. "Trust me. And get ready to fight!"

Hildr scoots up by my side, and Eir takes a few hurried steps to catch up, her face pale and worried-looking. We march up to the line of winged Valkyries and stop in the same circle. Except at the last second, I spin around to face the winged Valkyries, imitated by my friends.

The red dragon growls as we approach with spears and swords in our hands. She looks as though she's going to have a go at me, and I look deep into her eyes and shake my head. I take the chance, and I call up to her. "I'm here because of Ness."

A strange look crosses the dragon's face. Her lips seem to relax, but her teeth remain bared, and she has a look of uncertainty in her eyes.

It takes all my courage to peel my eyes from her, not knowing how she is going to react, and I stare at the winged Valkyries in front of us. The flying winged Valkyries lower and fall into line next to the standing winged Valkyries, their piercing blue eyes squinting with disdain.

With them all lined up against one another in their tan leather jackets and their medium-blue tight pants and their white shirts, it is a mission to tell the differences among them, except for the few stylish haircuts. Each winged Valkyrie has pure blond hair and a perfect complexion, and each one is almost the mirror image of the next. Even the mistress looks nearly as young as the Valkyries my age. Something hangs around Mistress Sigrun's neck, and I realize it is a dragon's-tooth necklace. She notices the direction of my gaze and clasps the chain with her spare hand, the one not holding the spear. Her eyes are wary, and annoyance flickers over her face. She pulls slightly at the dragon-tooth necklace and glances up at the red dragon then back at us.

"What is the meaning of this?" Mistress Sigrun's voice has the usual sneer reserved for wingless Valkyries. "You are supposed to be over here, fighting on our side against the dragon."

I stand tall. "I can't let you do it, Mistress. This dragon is already wounded and has already been fought against enough. And besides, this is barbaric. Dragons should not be treated like this."

She lifts her chin, still tugging at her necklace, and paces in front of us, using her spear like a staff, its end clicking against the hard surface of the ground. She glares at me from out of the corner of her eye. "You are young, wingless. You would not know what the past has held. It is hard for you to know exactly how old I am because my Valkyrie blessing removes all the lines that indicate my age, making me seem young. However, I am a much older Valkyrie, and I have been around for centuries. During that time, I have partaken in wars against the dragons. I have seen the devastation they cause and what they have done to the Valkyries in the past. They are cruel, malicious creatures. They deserve nothing more than to be fought against like this. In fact, they deserve a punishment much worse." She paces more, continuing to tug at her necklace. "Much blood was lost on both sides, and I was witness to this. I even partook in these battles, slaying a dragon of my own." She flicks the tooth toward me. "This is my trophy from that dragon."

I stare at the tooth in horror. That used to belong to a living thing, that piece that she wears around her neck, and she slaughtered it.

The mistress continues, "The horror and devastation was something I will not forget, and the dragons must be reminded of this. They must be reminded to keep to this alliance, and we must learn how to continue to fight against them in case they break our alliance and fight against us, causing us much death. Odin was also a witness to this. He supports this alliance one hundred percent. And you coming along and making friends with dragons—that is atrocious. You are wrecking all of our work from the past, rubbing our faces in the dirt of the memory. You show no respect for us as winged Valkyries. You were only given access to Midgard because you won that battle somehow. Well, by cheating, to be honest." She flicks her hand aside. "And today, I am giving you three the chance to prove to us that you are worth something on Asgard, as your worth is nothing on Midgard because you cannot reap souls." She raises her chin, and I want to wipe that smirk off her face.

"So this is your last chance. Turn around and fight with us, or you can go back to the academy." Mistress Sigrun returns to her original spot in the line of Valkyries, and several Valkyries take to the sky and flutter above the head of the dragon.

I peer over my shoulder at the dragon behind me, and her curious eyes are focused on me. I'm pretty sure by this gaze that she is the red dragon that I ran into when I was cleaning the stalls. This dragon hasn't been here long, and from her reaction to Ness's name, I believe that I have struck it right and she is Ness's daughter. I peer down at her chain and notice it has plenty of slack. The dragon could easily have charged forward and jumped on us from behind at any time, but she didn't. I fiddle with the spear in my hand, and I slam the end on the ground.

"Okay. You want us to fight with you, then that's what we will do." I notice in my peripheral vision that Hildr and Eir glance sideways at me, their faces full of confusion. I grin awkwardly, showing my teeth in a position that is almost a snarl, and I glance at each of them. Through my teeth, I say quietly, "Get ready." I look at Mistress Sigrun. I draw back my right leg before standing in the ready position with my sword aimed directly at them. I watch Mistress Sigrun's face turn into disdain and hate tainted with annoyance. The rocks clatter next to me as Hildr and Eir take up the same positions. The dragon snorts behind us, and a layer of smoke briefly covers us. I take that to mean she is with us.

I tilt my head to the side. "Bring it on!"

- CHAPTER SIX -

My heart pounds profusely, and my blood thumps in the veins of my throat. I almost hear the mistress scream at me over my defiance. I let the magic surge through my body. My strength is not at full capacity, but I'm not going to let that stop me. I'm healing by the minute, and I'll be restored to full strength soon. The winged Valkyries position themselves with their arrows, swords, and spears facing us and the dragon. I don't even know what the dragon's name is, but I'm ready to fight for her, and I can tell Hildr and Eir feel the same.

"What are you doing?" Eir whispers through her teeth. "I couldn't defeat three on top of the mountain. How do you propose I defeat at least thirty?"

"You forget it was the thirty that we were against on the mountain." I don't try to hide my spite.

She shakes her head. "Not initially, no. It was only three of them. The rest joined in after I fell off the side of the cliff."

"That's the way I remember it," Hildr says on the other side of me. "But even though I failed that fight, I'm not giving up on this one."

"You guys are good fighters. Stop stressing over it and just do it," I hiss through my teeth.

Eir squats lower and readies herself, resolve passing over her face.

I focus my attention on the winged Valkyries and call out, "You need to stop hurting the dragons."

Mistress Sigrun chuckles. "As if that's going to happen. They're one of our natural enemies. We have to learn how to fight against them."

"You could just be kind to them and use them as one of our allies instead," I say.

Her chuckle rises an octave, piercing the air. "Oh, you're such a dreamer." Her amusement is pushed aside by a scowl. "Fight them!" Immediately, the winged Valkyries swoop down, swiping swords and aiming spears at us or the dragon behind us. Once again, their unfairness is manifested, but I'm not going to focus on that. I beckon my magic to gather as I strike back, dodge spears, and block swinging swords with mine. I hold my palm out to them, and I can feel the magic ready and loaded.

Mistress Sigrun's eyes drop to the swirl in the middle of my palm, and her face streaks with terror before it's quickly pushed aside.

"If you don't stop fighting us, I'm going to let this fly." I stretch my palm out farther to indicate what I mean, although I'm pretty sure by the looks on their faces, they already know. The magic burns some more in my palm, beckoning to be released, especially when I aim it straight at Mistress Sigrun.

"I would stop if I were you. I've been practicing this." I let a little magic shoot at a pile of rocks, and they scatter everywhere. The winged Valkyries jump. Their wings flitter, and a couple of them lose feathers. They pause their fighting to survey the scene.

Mistress Sigrun's face indicates that she is pushing aside her fear once again. Determination sets in her eyes, and she lifts her chin. "If you use your magic, then you are just proving that you're weaker than us. And that you cannot fight."

Hildr cackles. "I don't know how you think she can be weaker if she holds powerful magic.

That's something only a dumb person would say."

Mistress Sigrun narrows her eyes at her. "Very well, then. Let's do this!"

The winged Valkyries fly at us again from all directions, and I release my power at them, amazed at how quickly they can dodge a flying bullet and manage to flick themselves out of the way by a hair's width, allowing the magic to bypass them.

"You know, we have also been training against magic users in case we come up against someone like you," the mistress sneers.

My curiosity is piqued, but I'll have to leave my questions for later.

"Perhaps it is because I am hesitant to hurt you that you are actually being missed. I don't like hurting people or other beings," I say. "Did you ever think of that?"

I shoot some more magic, and it barely misses the Valkyries. I have to learn to aim in the direction that they are going, not directly at them, but there is some truth in what I told the mistress. A thump sounds in front of me, and a roar resounds as golden scales start to appear, forming into the shape of Elan. She has landed directly between the Valkyries and us. My heart fills with pride, and I'm so happy to see her. Either Elan was watching, or somehow she's heard the commotion. Something thuds on the left of me, and I look over to see Drogon has landed next to Hildr. Another lighter thud rattles the ground on my other side, and Naga has landed next to Eir. The dragons' shoulders are pulled back, and their wings are spread wide, making them look more intimidating. All three of them roar, and the roar of the red dragon behind me joins them. Elan spins around and sets her tail free, wiping out a few of the Valkyries on the ground.

Mistress Sigrun manages to flap a few times and barely manages to get out of the road in time. When she recovers, she says, "I see you brought your dragon. Good. We can practice against her too."

The blood drains from my skin. "No. I don't want Elan to get hurt." The red dragon barges past us, narrowly missing us with her large feet. Her clasp clatters on a rock as it remains secured around her back ankle, but her chain is broken. I frown in confusion. I could have sworn that the chain was secured not long ago. I don't have time to work out what happened, but I'm glad that she has decided to take our side. The red dragon stands next to Elan. She pushes her head forward and bellows. It's almost as though she received a second wind from seeing Elan in this group.

A strange sensation captures my attention, and I search for it. It feels like magic, but it can't be my magic because it doesn't feel like that to me. It makes me think that perhaps the dark elf is watching us from somewhere in the background. I briefly search the horizon, confident enough to do this now that I have four dragons standing in front of us. Something charges across the top of the mountain in the distance. I wonder if it is the dark elf. I don't know why he would be spying on us. Then, out of the corner of my eye, I think I see another shadow or something darting by, and I search the top of a different mountain. That doesn't seem right. Unless the dark elf can teleport, there are at least two of them running around up there. This is cause for alarm.

Something winces in front of me, pulling my attention back to the group. Naga has been injured by one of the spears. The Valkyrie steps forward to retrieve it. I shoot her with magic, and she collapses to the ground, unconscious, her feet thrusting a few times before they fall still. I run up to Naga, and Eir is already there.

"Naga, are you okay?" I place a hand on his side.

He nods.

Yes, Naga okay. Thank you. Naga will heal. Forget Naga. Now time to fight. The pain disappears from his eyes, and he puts on a brave face.

"I couldn't forget you, Naga. But I will fight by your side, and hopefully, you will heal soon."

Elan scoops down and picks up the Valkyrie in her mouth and flicks her aside. The Valkyrie's wings awkwardly flitter as they blow against the wind, and she flops on the ground. Elan was tossing her aside to get away from the circle.

I shoot some magic and hit some more Valkyries. They fall to the ground, unconscious. Elan does the same thing by picking them up and throwing them to the side, their comatose bodies looking almost humorous as they are cast off like stuffed dolls.

With four dragons lined up against the thirty winged trainee Valkyries, Mistress Sigrun's face lacks confidence, her insecurity evidently growing with each winged Valkyrie who flies unconscious in the other direction.

There is nothing she can do. Their weapons against the four dragons and the three wingless Valkyries, one wielding magic, are no competition.

The mistress pushes backward and lifts into the air, retreating from the position with her hands held high. "Stop, Valkyries!" Eyes glower down at me. "I deem this an unfair fight. I refuse to fight in these circumstances. You may retreat."

Each of the winged Valkyries imitates Mistress Sigrun and pushes backward, flying away from the dragons. That is, except for the ones Elan tossed, as they still lie unconscious, a couple of them with broken wings.

The four dragons snarl victoriously as they watch the Valkyries retreat. Mistress Sigrun's face sours as she hovers in the air not far from us.

I stare at her, not feeling intimidated yet wondering what she's going to do next.

Suddenly, something flies through the air and hits her in the back. Her face drops, and her body flings forward like a rag doll, somersaulting toward the dragon.

"Elan!" I cry out. "Do something!" I can tell Mistress Sigrun is in trouble, and I know that my small frame is helpless to stop her fall. Despite my annoyance with Mistress Sigrun, I don't want her harmed.

Without questioning me, Elan dives forward, spreading her wings, and she lines one of them up directly in front of where the mistress will fall. She breaks the hard landing with the inside of her wing, cushioning the fall like a soft net. Elan topples backward as the mistress's body hits, and she cradles her softly. Eir gasps as Elan narrowly misses her. I search the area, looking for what might have caused the mistress to fall like that. I scan the mountains behind the mistress, where I had seen the images before, and where I thought I'd seen the dark elf. Surely he wouldn't want to harm Mistress Sigrun, but I can never be sure.

- CHAPTER SEVEN -

As I scan the mountaintops in the distance, I think I see something dart behind a boulder. I fix my attention on that area, looking for any sign of movement, when something catches my eye from the other mountain.

I can't make out the image in the distance. The Valkyries run toward Elan, and their eyes dart up apprehensively, searching for their mistress.

Elan stretches her wing, showing off the mistress lying within its membrane. The red dragon tucks her head in front of the Valkyries, blocking their way, and releases a long snarl from the pit of her throat. The Valkyries stop in their tracks and stare at Ness's daughter, their eyes wide as they retreat a few paces. The red dragon huffs out a large plume of steam, causing the Valkyries to back up quicker, their eyes never leaving her except for the occasional flick to Mistress Sigrun to make sure she's okay. Elan slowly tilts her wing downward, letting the mistress slide softly to the ground, her wings flopping lifelessly around her and partially covering her. The Valkyries' faces are full of confusion, and they glare at me as though I have attacked her.

"You! You did this!" Rota accuses me. Her arm shakes as she points her sword at me, her knuckles turning white from her firm grasp of the hilt.

I laugh with disbelief. "You're kidding, right?" I shake my head. "You of all people should know that my magic doesn't pull. She was flung as though hit from behind. It was because of me that Elan caught her. Now, why would I do that if I caused her this damage?"

Rota's eyes flick from side to side, as though looking for reassurance from Prima and Mist, but they look just as confused.

Another movement catches my eye on top of the mountain, and I gaze up. A figure stands next to a large boulder. The figure's arms move as though it is conjuring something. I point at it, warning the winged Valkyries that something is behind them. The Valkyries flinch as though I'm about to strike them, and my words are fraught with disbelief. It takes a moment to pull myself together. I attempt to turn their attention from me to the figure on the mountain. I am about to speak when I see something fly our way. Instinctively, I raise a barrier to stop whatever it is flying toward me.

Hildr, Eir, and their dragons remain within the protective barrier, and Ness's daughter joins them. I push the barrier farther until it protects all the Valkyries standing behind me. My recent practice with the Gilroma in the cave is proving useful—other than stopping a mountain from toppling on me. I marvel at the barrier as it blocks the magic, bouncing its potency away from my fellow students and the dragons. Whatever magic the strike held, it was rolling off the sides of my barrier into the ground around the base of its protection, not far from the outskirts of the winged Valkyries. They jump and flinch as the ground explodes into dust at the base of the barrier from the impact. After observing the hole in the ground behind them, they stare accusingly at me as though I had caused this instead of defending both them and my friends from damage. They raise their weapons and look as though they're about to attack us.

I stare at them in disbelief. "That wasn't me."

Rota stares at me, and she calls out, "Then why did the magic come from your direction?"

"It didn't come from my direction. It bounced off my protection barrier. The magic came from behind you. There is something on the mountains." I wave my other hand directly at the mountains. Their resolve wavers as a look of thoughtfulness crosses their faces. This quickly turns into action as another hit of magic comes our way. I raise a barrier just in time, and it explodes behind them, spraying the winged Valkyries with the dirt from the closer attack. "See. I told you it wasn't me."

Rota's face blanches, and she spins around and stares at the mountain. Suddenly, I'm faced with a sea of white as each winged Valkyrie imitates her and faces the mountain, and their wings face our direction.

One of the winged Valkyries flops to the ground, creating a small gap between those in the standoff. Through the gap, I see a figure not far from us at ground level. He looks like a dark elf that I once saw pictured in a book in the library. His long dark hair is pulled back into a ponytail, unlike Gilroma's. His ears point out and up from the side of his head, and his frame is tall and thin. He is dressed in armor, a sword clinging to his side. Although I see only the lone figure, he approaches slowly with surefooted confidence.

The sea of white wings in front of me back up slowly and part as they go around me to retreat behind the dragons and myself. I watch in disbelief. These are supposed to be our fearless warriors.

Realizing that the dragons and I are at the forefront of the battle, I refocus my attention on the distance, and several of these similarly dressed elves are approaching, each tall and with a different color of hair. They form one unbroken line, and I estimate that there are fifty marching forward. Their swords are clanging against their metal armor in a synchronized march.

We need a strong leader to combat these elves successfully. I gaze down at unconscious Mistress Sigrun, and it is clear we will not have a competent leader. Searching around me, I try to judge who would be the best leader out of these winged Valkyries. They have seen several more battles than Hildr, Eir, or I have. My eyes land on one of the senior students—a winged Valkyrie in her final year. She must've sensed the responsibility had fallen on her shoulders, and her hesitant eyes glance at the unconscious mistress. Her face contorts before being ironed expressionless, and seconds later, she steps forward as though taking the lead. Although she is trying to hide it, I can see her attempt to pull herself together while observing the fifty elves in front of us. She lifts her arm high, holding up her spear, and bellows, "Get ready! We will defend Asgard!" She shakes her spear in the air a few times.

Several of the winged Valkyries join her, standing in a line just past me and outside the line my barrier had reached before. After several Valkyries join the line, they raise their spears and swords and call in unison, "We are ready!" They shake their weapons threateningly. The fighting call of the Valkyries pierces the air with a loud trill, and I flinch, fighting the urge to cover my ears. I look up just in time to see something fly through the air and hit the new Valkyrie leader squarely in the chest, flinging her backward and slamming her onto the flank of Drogon. Her body slides down his side and falls unconscious to the ground. Drogon's brown eyes widen in shock as he peers down at her still form.

- CHAPTER EIGHT -

With a look of destruction plastered on his face, the elf and his comrades approach. He pauses with his legs a shoulder width apart, his eyes never leaving us. "Stand aside, Valkyries," he calls across the distance. "I have come for Odin and his palace. Stand aside, and you shall reign in Asgard with us."

It takes me a minute to realize our group is blocking his way to the palace. It lies in a valley not far from the academy. But then I think, he has some nerve. Does he really expect the Valkyries to stand aside? Protecting Asgard and building a strong army from Midgard's warriors is everything that Valkyries live for. If any of them step aside, then they will be de-winged and disgraced because they have betrayed their realm and their one job in life.

The dark elf's chin lifts slightly higher than normal, and arrogance radiates from him. I keep my peripheral vision peeled on the white wings of the Valkyries lined up slightly in front of me. I'm determined to watch and see if any of them move. At the same time, I mentally prepare myself for a fight, hoping that Elan is doing the same.

A flicker of white flashes in the corner of my left eye. I turn, ignoring the clamminess on my face as I wonder whether a Valkyrie is about to stand aside. But as I stare at her, I realize it is just a flicker of annoyance manifesting in her white wings. Her feet don't move an inch.

The dark elf moves suddenly, flicking an arm at the next leader of the Valkyries, his magic colliding with her and knocking her backward. She crashes against the flank of the red dragon. Ness's daughter snarls at the Valkyrie then backs away before she turns toward the dark elf and growls at him. I am sure the snarl at the Valkyrie was purely because of how this Valkyrie had treated her not long before. She nudges the Valkyrie away with her front feet, clearing her path to the elf. The Valkyrie flops around lifelessly, her wings falling in all directions.

A strange twitching travels along the line of winged Valkyries. It looks as though they are nervous and the twitching is a manifestation of their uncertainty about how to deal with magic. The academy Valkyries haven't had to defend themselves against this.

The next senior Valkyrie calls out, "Why don't you fight us like real warriors and not hide behind your magic?"

One side of the dark elf's mouth lifts in a sneer. "But then what fun would that be? We wouldn't have a guarantee of winning. You want to challenge us to the brute force of a fight?" He seems to feign feeling insecure and upset. "Oh no, perhaps we might fall to your mighty swords. You might actually defeat us." He pulls out his sword. "Unlikely! But I'm willing to let you think you have a chance." He raises his sword in the air and cries, "Charge!"

A deafening cry echoes across the plain as they charge forward, swords held in their hands and armor clanking as it collides with other armor between their running legs.

The winged Valkyries release a higher-pitched cry as they run forward. The three Valkyries hit by magic remain unconscious on the ground near us. I watch the charging Valkyries, then I turn to Eir, Hildr, and the dragons. "We need to help them. There must be at least another twenty of them. The odds are not in our favor. As much as I don't like the winged Valkyries, we can't let Asgard fall."

We'll help, Elan says. *Won't we?* She glances at the other dragons, and they slowly nod. *My mother told me that there was a time that the dark elves ruled the dragons. This was a very dark time for the dragons. There wasn't an alliance agreement. As much as the winged Valkyries mistreat their captors, there is an alliance, and we can mostly live in peace. Hopefully, Mother is working on a better agreement.*

The red dragon snarls.

Thank you, Tanda. Elan doesn't hide her excitement. *Your cooperation is appreciated. Drogon?*

Drogon echoes his agreement. When Elan looks at Naga, he lifts his head high then tiptoes on the spot from one foot to the other. It almost looks like a dance. He throws his head forward and growls, exposing his teeth.

"Oh, you're so cute, Naga!" Eir chuckles, and Naga glances appreciatively at her, giving her a toothy smile that looks cheeky, unlike Elan's aggressive grin.

Then let's stop them! Tanda snarls, turning the mood serious again.

Let's go! Elan turns invisible, and the ground rumbles around me before rocks scatter backward followed by a big gush of wind. I am sure she has pushed off into the air. The sound of wings flapping confirms my assumptions.

"Be careful, Elan," I call to the empty sky.

You, too, Kara.

I turn to Hildr and Eir, and the determination on Hildr's face matches her spiky red hair. Her green eyes are set, and her hand twitches over her sword hilt. "Finally! We finally get to fight alongside the winged Valkyries against a common enemy." Giving in to her itch, she reaches for her sword and yanks it out, the metal sliding against metal, and she charges forward, lining up with the other Valkyries. "We finally get to do something noble," she calls over her shoulder.

Eir watches Hildr. Her face shows concern. "I wish there were a peaceful solution, but I can't find one."

"Then join us, Eir," I say.

We stare at the dragons flying above, and when a cry catches my attention, I gaze across the field. Dark elves are flung to the side, their faces confused as an invisible force captures their body.

"Are you coming?" I ask Eir.

She nods, and we run forward until we're in line with the winged Valkyries. Hildr's fingers fiddle with her sword hilt as she eyes the dark elves in the distance. With my sword in hand, I weave through the Valkyries toward her side, and Eir is entering the line on her other side.

Elves attack us in one formation, their swords raised high. An elf charges at me, swinging his sword directly at my throat, and I block it with my sword. Clanging metal sounds throughout the air, hurting my eardrums. He pulls his sword back and strikes again. I twist, narrowly missing it as I swing my sword to the opposite side. He manages to retreat just in time to block my strike, and his sword clashes with the edge of mine. A chip of metal springs to the side. My stomach sinks as I glance at my sword and spot a slight chip in the blade. The Elven sword must be made of much stronger metal. This is not good. I wonder how many other Valkyries have already faced the same problem.

He attacks with his sword aiming straight for my torso. I pull in my stomach and jump back, blocking it with my sword. When I realize I'm in the clear, I glance over to another Valkyrie on the side, and I take a look at their sword. It is also dented all the way up its length. At this rate, I don't think it will be long before some of the Valkyries' swords break. There are so many more of them than us, and their swords are stronger, not to mention that they also have magic. We are only students of the Valkyrie Academy. We aren't full-fledged

Valkyries like the many mature ones who go off to battle. When the winged Valkyries from the academy go to battle, they are more like rookies going for their first day—always overseen by a senior Valkyrie. And our senior Valkyrie, Mistress Sigrun, lies unconscious in a crumpled heap several yards behind us.

I hear the slight whistling of the wind as a sword swings toward me again. I dart in the opposite direction while swinging my sword and blocking the blow. My ear screams as the metal clangs. I'm suddenly overcome with a strange sensation. Something is buzzing in the air. That something reminds me of what I felt earlier yet couldn't place. I wonder if it was these elves that I could sense before. Besides Gilroma, who is encouraging my magic and training me, I have not met another dark elf and did not know that I could sense them.

The strange buzzing grows stronger. I don't know whether any of the other Valkyries can sense it or if only I sense it because of the magic within me. Something must be amiss, because the sensation suddenly surges.

The sword swings at me again, aiming for my throat, and I manage to block it, costing my sword another chip. While holding the block, for a split second, I let my eyes travel, looking for what may be causing the sensation, and my eyes land on the chief dark elf. His hand is weaving and darting around, as though conjuring up something like the elf on the mountaintop not long before. His hand weaves some more, and I sense the magic building. He twirls it a few more times and pulls it back then aims straight for Hildr.

I hear the whistling sound of the dark elf's sword in front of me, swinging for me again. I move my sword quickly, spinning, and block its blow. I lift my hand, then I dive toward Hildr, forcing out my palm and shooting my magic out and around Hildr to try to block the blow. I'm not sure if this will work, but I've got to try.

- CHAPTER NINE -

The blow lands against my magic. I can feel it, and a small jolt of excitement mixed with relief runs through my veins. My barrier managed to block the blow against Hildr just in time. A bright light sparks off the blow, and Hildr blinks. Her face expresses disbelief as she stares precisely where the bright lights flashed only inches away from her. When the recognition hits, her eyes widen, and she turns her head until her uncertain eyes land on me. When she spots my outreached palm, her face relaxes. "Thank you!" she quickly mutters before she embraces her sword with both hands and slices it through the barrier, cutting the torso of the dark elf in front of her.

He lurches forward, his hand grasping the injured spot, and it is only seconds later that his body lurches farther forward as he's pulled up into the air by an invisible force and thrown to the side.

Drogon lands next to Hildr, his eyes agitated and vicious. As he stares toward the dark elves, he thumps his tail on the ground. He stares into Hildr's eyes for a moment, and I can only imagine the private conversation they are having. He leans in sideways, as though making sure Hildr avoids his many horns, and she presses toward him, embracing his nose as he nuzzles her. She casts me a glance then climbs up his side and onto his back, hanging onto his horns and scales. Drogon takes to the sky, rising to a decent height after a few wing beats. He then nosedives toward a few dark elves while Hildr hooks her legs around his neck and grasps her sword. At the last second, Drogon twists, and Hildr drags her sword along several dark elves, a cry of victory following her as she slices four of them along their backs. They cry out, and their knees buckle while they drop their swords on the ground beside them.

Eir squeals in delight and claps her hands. "Good on you, Hildr!"

I turn to watch my back and notice the dark elf is closing in on me again. At the same time, Eir is calling out to Hildr and has drummed up the attention of the dark elves, and two of them corner her. Several distressed Valkyrie cries ring throughout the air, and shivers run up my spine.

Ignoring them, I turn to block the blow of the approaching dark elf, and a big gush of wind surfaces behind me. I spin in time to see a dark elf behind me being dragged up into the sky by an invisible force. I gasp in relief. Elan has grabbed him and flung him to the side.

I about-face just in time to see the dark elf on the ground next to me using this distraction to strike another blow. I dodge in the nick of time, not having enough notice to raise my sword to fight back. The dark elf swings at me again. I maneuver, so he misses me, striking my sword in his direction and letting out a groan of frustration as it misses him.

As I spin, I spot Eir being attacked by two dark elves. I recognize the sensation of the drawing of magic, and I look for the culprit. At the same time, I have to remind myself to swing at this dark elf who is still pursuing me. I swing my sword, he evades it easily, and another frustrated groan escapes my mouth. *Why can't he just fall already?*

The magic builds, and I follow its pull, filled with dread since the sensation is coming from an area near Eir. She just manages to avoid the blows from the two dark elves. I study them, but they are still attacking her, and there is no indication of them pulling from a magic force. But I can't shake the feeling stemming from that direction. Eir swings her sword, blocking the blow of one of the dark elves' strikes. She dances to the side as the second elf strikes. He narrowly misses her, yet his movement has opened space, and another dark elf is on the other side of him, his hand weaving magic just like the last—circling and spinning as though he is building the magic. He draws his hand back, and I throw my palm out, sending out the magic as fast as I can, blocking his blow from Eir as he flings it at her. My barrier spreads right as his magic reaches not far from Eir's face, and the bright light explodes inches in front of Eir's eyes. I breathe a sigh of relief, and my shoulders cave from the ease of pressure. I catch sight of Eir's face as she realizes what has happened and relief washes over her.

A flash of blue falls from the sky, and I dart sideways as the blue streak knocks the magic-wielding dark elf to the side. It then changes direction abruptly and bowls over the two dark elves attacking Eir. Their swords are knocked out of their hands and land on the ground with a clang. At the same time, the blue streak knocks away all immediate threats from Eir.

Something clangs behind me, and I spin around in time to see another dark elf flop to the ground, the sword in his hand held high as though he's ready to attack. He collapses face-first onto the hard ground with a spear sticking out of his back. The void behind him fills with the exhausted face of Mistress Sigrun. Her skin is wan, and it is clear that it has taken all her strength to raise her arms above her head and thrust her spear into the dark elf's back. I'm not sure what to think. It is too hard to process that my mean-hearted mistress actually protected me from a blow. That is one move I never expected to see from the academy mistress, the hater of wingless Valkyries. Her face turns paler as she drops to her knees.

"Don't think too much of it, wingless." Her backside drops to her heels. "It was purely an act of survival. You have the magic. You are the only one who can protect us from these magic-wielding creeps." She holds her hand over her chest as she huffs, trying to catch her breath. "That is the only reason." Her shoulders sag.

Suddenly, I realize what I must do. I charge for the center of the line of fighting Valkyries.

"Valkyries, fall in line!" I call, flinging my sword to the ground.

Several clanks of swords surround me before Rota calls out, "Why should we fall in next to you?"

"Just do it," I hiss through my teeth. "I know you can't stand me, but now is not the time for this."

Mistress Sigrun's soft voice calls from behind, "Just do it, Valkyries."

They cast several disbelieving looks over their shoulders at the deflated mistress sitting on her heels before they slowly fall in line.

Once they are lined up, I focus on the current of magic deep within me, pulling it from every corner of my body. Raising my hands, I set my mind on the path of destruction and let the magic pour out of me from the very depths of my soul, picturing my intentions. I can feel the barrier rising between the Valkyries and the dark elves. I raise it higher to combat any strike of magic or a blow of a sword or any other weapon. The frustration is evident on the dark elves' faces as they continually bang their weapons against my barrier, unable to penetrate its protection. Amusement dances under my skin as I watch individual elves being picked up and flung sideways and away from our area by the invisible force of Elan. The elves are joined by Tanda and Drogon, with Hildr calling war cries from Drogon's back.

A dark elf aims his magic toward Hildr, and I cry, "Look out, Hildr!"

Drogon dodges sideways, and the blast of magic skims past her head as he flips in the opposite direction, Hildr struggling to hang on and slipping sideways on his back. I seriously have to get to work and get them to make at least some straps if not a saddle. She manages to grasp one of the many horns protruding from his head and straightens her sitting position when Drogon corrects his path.

A blue streak flies in, aiming straight at the elf who threw the magic, and I watch, fascinated, as it collides with the elf, sending him catapulting into the air before landing solidly on the ground. The elf's face is frozen in an expression of disbelief.

Something switches, and a strange look washes over each elf's face before they slowly back away. I'm not sure what to think. *Are they planning something, perhaps a different kind of attack? Are they leaving?*

A loud trumpet blast sounds behind us, and I allow myself to peek over my shoulder. I see a large flock of white wings as Valkyries fly over the hillside with weapons in hand. The senior Valkyries have finally come. Word must've gotten out somehow. It seems ironic that they arrive now, as the fight is starting to favor our side. The Valkyries fly down and land beside us, closing in on the dark elves.

Meanwhile, the dark elves continue to dissipate after being shaken and thrown to the side, blood pouring from their torsos. Despite the arrival of the senior Valkyries, the dragons continue their attack. A bloody battle erupts until the last dark elf has been removed from Asgard, either slain or escaped.

- CHAPTER TEN -

"Mistress Sigrun! Since when do you fight with dragons and wingless Valkyries?" A Valkyrie lands in front of our mistress. She crosses her arms while glaring down at her.

Mistress Sigrun's mouth drops open, her face filled with shock as she stares up at the confronting Valkyrie. She crisply says, "I do not work with wingless Valkyries or dragons.

This has turned out completely different from the plan."

The Valkyrie folds her wings and taps her foot. "What do you mean? I would like you to elaborate."

Mistress Sigrun rises to her feet, one leg at a time, her mouth groaning her body's protest. "This was meant to be a routine practice battle against the red dragon. It all started as usual, and I thought I would teach these three wingless Valkyries a lesson. For quite some time, they have *insisted* they are just as good as the winged Valkyries, and I thought I would prove them wrong and put them in their rightful place."

"And how did you expect to execute this?" The Valkyrie lifts her nose.

"By making them fight against the dragon. You see, these three have become *friends* with three of these dragons. The plan was wrecked when the wingless refused to fight against the dragon, and the dragons came and crashed our little battle against the red dragon. Instead, they decided to protect it and fight on the dragon's side." The mistress straightens her shoulders and glares my way. "We had this under control until the dark elves came, and it was then that magic was involved and dragons dived in and protected the Valkyries. They wanted to protect their wingless counterparts first, and the wingless were determined to butt their noses in our battle, even though we would have easily defeated the dark elves without their help."

I roll my eyes. Here we go again. The mistress is taking all the credit. I lose interest as the mistress ignores my disbelief and continues. My gaze wanders up to the hill from where the senior Valkyries came, where a few of them remain. A black figure in the middle of them captures my attention. I squint at the figure. It's Loki. I can't believe it. What is the god of mischief and the being behind the zmey doing with the Valkyries? I must confront him and find out about the dragon-egg stealing.

The mistress's voice drones in the background as I charge up the hill.

"I never thought I would see any of this, but life has turned crazy lately. This particular Valkyrie and her friends challenge everything we have been led to believe about the wingless Valkyries." She points a finger in my direction.

"Where do you think you're going?" The senior Valkyrie's voice is harsh. "Hey, wingless!" I spin around to find the winged Valkyrie staring at me, her eyes glaring. "What is the meaning of you calling the dragons friends?"

I raise my chin. "I will not fight against the dragons. If you make them friends instead of enemies, they could be great allies in the war and will battle against anything trying to harm Asgard. Even though dragons do not like the winged Valkyries, they stood up for Asgard and, in this case, helped us win the battle. So much so that we were already starting to take control of the battle before you arrived… as much as we appreciate your help." I throw that in at the last second. It was nice not having to finish the battle completely, and I guess it was an attempt to butter her up slightly.

The winged Valkyrie does not answer me. Instead, she turns to face the mistress, her face a beacon of displeasure. "And what of this magic you talk about?"

Again Mistress Sigrun points her finger at me. "It is her. She is the one who wields it. She is cursed, I tell you. She has brought nothing but misery to our academy over the last few years. And this misery has escalated since she has wielded magic."

My mouth drops open. "Are you serious? We just saved you and your Valkyries. We stopped them from attacking you. Blocking them and their advantage of having the power of magic. If it weren't for me, you would all have been struck down in moments and most likely slaughtered before the senior Valkyries came over the hill."

Mistress Sigrun glares at me. "It is bad enough that you have managed to earn your way into entering Midgard. But now you are expecting to be treated as a warrior in Asgard. You are a persistent nuisance in Midgard, and now you're a nuisance in Asgard. Now leave my sight before I demand the senior Valkyries arrest you and lock you up in Odin's castle."

I gaze at Mistress Sigrun in disbelief. I can't believe her. I have done so much for Asgard and now for the Valkyries. Yet I'm still told that I am useless and a pain.

Someone grabs my arm from behind, and I turn to see Eir's sympathetic face staring at me. She pulls on my arm again. "Come on, Kara. Let's go."

A loud thud sounds not far from us, and Hildr climbs down off Drogon's back, furiously glaring at Mistress Sigrun. She calls to the mistress. "You should be dead! She should have left you at the mercy of all those dark elves. If it weren't for Kara and our help, you, along with most of your Valkyries, would be injured or dead right now." She grunts and shakes her fist at her then stomps toward me. "Come on. Let's go."

Elan lands in front of me, her golden scales slowly growing visible. The senior Valkyrie gasps and grabs her sword, her eyes never leaving Elan. "She's an emperor dragon, the most dangerous kind!"

"I know." My voice is calm as I reach up and touch Elan's nose. She nudges into my hand. "Thank you for your help, Elan. It's been wonderful. Please take the dragons back to where they are meant to go."

Elan looks at the Valkyrie and Mistress Sigrun, her eyes narrowing. She huffs and covers them in hot steam. The two Valkyries back away. *Would you like me to take them and plunk them somewhere inconvenient? You know, like in the middle of the dragon wilderness? I wouldn't mind. Really, I wouldn't. It would almost be my pleasure.* Her lips part in a vicious grin.

I chuckle softly. "No, thank you, Elan." I stroke her nose. "As much as that thought pleases me, I will not be nasty to them. I still hope that one day, they will see us differently. I have to live among these Valkyries."

Not if they are planted in the middle of the wilderness, you don't. You know, far away from here. Her toothy grin widens.

I chuckle then rest my forehead against her snout before pulling back. "I'll see you later."

Elan huffs dramatically. *If that's what you really want. Last offer!*

"Thanks, Elan. But I need you to watch over these three dragons. Tanda is free, and you need to make sure she understands the conditions of her freedom and how it will affect the alliance."

Elan rolls her eyes. *Okay! Always the serious one.*

She pushes into the air, and the three dragons follow her, returning to their stalls of their own free will—but not without Tanda glancing over her shoulder and giving me a strange look. It isn't a vicious look but more of a curious glance, and I hope this is a step in the right direction for her as well. I hope this means that another dragon is on our side— despite the fact that her mother wanted to eat me.

Remembering Loki up on the hill, I glance that way only to be disappointed. He's gone. There is no sign of him among the white feathers of the Valkyries. I expel a loud breath. I will have to try to find him another time. I wonder whether my thirst for answers will ever be quenched.

Reluctantly, I walk with Hildr and Eir to our dormitory. I strip off my weapons and throw them on my bed. "I could use a shower."

"Me too," Eir agrees, wincing as her fingers get caught in her long brown strands of hair.

"Yeah, I feel pretty much like a dirty, muddy cesspool of blood, sweat, and dirt." The freckles on Hildr's nose clump together as she screws it up.

Eir grimaces. "Hildr!"

"What? That's how I feel. Just think of all the stuff we have been covered in."

I head to the shower, afterward changing into a fresh set of leathers. I don't feel like going back to class right now, but it is part of my curriculum at the academy. No matter what we face, we are to return to ordinary lessons straightaway. I throw my old leathers to the side in my laundry pile. I will have to wash them shortly, or else they will stink, especially after today's effort. I search for my shoes and strap them up, and Hildr and Eir do the same. I pull the leather straps tight and tie them, ready for another class. I rise to my feet and head to the door. "Are you guys rea—"

I collide with a figure standing in front of me. I glance around, surprised. "Rota!" Her face looks almost as shocked as I feel.

Hildr jumps to her feet. "What are you doing here? The nerve!" She stomps a few steps toward Rota. "You need to leave now! You're not welcome in our room." She plants her hands firmly on her hips.

Resignation crosses Rota's face, and her eyes flick to the ground. "I know." She looks at Hildr, then Eir, then back at me. Her face has a strange, puzzled look that I've never seen before. She lifts her arms, and it's clear she holds something. I glance down, only to be overcome with shock. It's my sword. Well, I think it's my sword. Now it is polished and looks almost brand-new. Every single dent from the fight has been worked out. The end of the hilt is adorned with a set of wings. At the base of the hilt, right before the blade, is another set of metal wings. My mouth drops open. The sword is beautiful.

"I found this on the battlefield. I know it's yours, and I know how much trouble you will get into if the senior Valkyries realize it is yours. So I picked it up and polished it. I also worked out the dents with a grinder." An awkward silence fills the room. "And I added a few ornaments. I hope you like it." She runs her finger across the edge of the sword, and a small trickle of blood runs down her finger as she pulls it away. "It's really sharp now. Not as blunt as it used to be."

I reach out and take it from her, not sure what to say. "Thank you."

She smiles sympathetically. "I think you deserve it. You have done much for the winged Valkyries. Even though you have used your magic on me, I know I deserved it. I hope you take this as a peace offering." She shoves the sword into my hands, then she exits the door without another word.

The End

ACKNOWLEDGMENTS

I am touched by the enormous amount of support I have received from my immediate family. My husband has been a helpful first reader and at times been a wonderful motivator, with hints of ideas to help me through the blanks. The support from my three sons has also been overwhelming. They have put up with my head being in the clouds, thinking about the next plot twist or story for several years. Along with many hours spent working on my books and keeping in touch with my readers.

A big thank you to my extended family who support me being a book enthusiast.

A huge thank you to my editor, Angela M., her editing and writing tips, and my Proofreader, Virge B., for picking up the things we missed.

Thank you to all of my readers who have loved my work, and continue to read my stories. I would love for you to share your thoughts in a review on one or all of the following:

Amazon.com
Goodreads
Barnes & Noble
You can follow Katrina Cope at:

https://www.facebook.com/Author.Katrina.Cope

https://twitter.com/Katrina_R_Cope

https://www.goodreads.com/author/show/7265107.Katrina_Cope

https://www.katrinacopebooks.com

http://http://www.amazon.com/Katrina-Cope/e/B00F00JF9M/

Book 7 of Valkyrie Academy Dragon Alliance Series 'Warned' released November 2019.

BOOKS BY KATRINA COPE

~~~~~

Pre-Teen Books

THE SANCTUM SERIES

JAYDEN'S CYBERMOUNTAIN

SCARLET'S ESCAPE

TAYLOR'S PLIGHT

ERIC & THE BLACK AXES

ADRIANNA'S SURGE

~~~~~

Young Adult Urban Fantasy

AFTERLIFE SERIES

FLEDGLING

THE TAKING

ANGELIC RETRIBUTION

DIVIDED PATHS

Afterlife Novelette

THE GATEKEEPER

~~~~~

Young Adult Urban Paranormal Fantasy

SUPERNATURAL EVOLVEMENT SERIES

(Associated with the Afterlife Series)

WITCH'S LEGACY (#0.5 Prequel)

AALIYAH

~~~~~

Young Adult Fantasy Nordic Myths

VALKYRIE ACADEMY DRAGON ALLIANCE

SERIES

MARKED (Prequel)

CHOSEN

VANISHED

SCORNED

INFLICTED

EMPOWERED

AMBUSHED

WARNED

ABDUCTED

GET UPDATES & NOTIFICATIONS OF GIVEAWAYS

Would you like a FREE copy of Marked?
Visit here:
https://www.katrinacopebooks.com/valkyrie-academy-dragon-alliance
Through this link you can sign up for my newsletter and receive a FREE copy of Marked plus updates about my fantasy books, sales and notification of giveaways.

DID YOU ENJOY THIS BOOK?
YOU CAN MAKE A BIG DIFFERENCE.

Honest reviews of my books help bring them to the attention of other readers.

If you've enjoyed this book, I'd be grateful if you could spend a few minutes leaving a review (it can be as short as you like).
The review can be left on Amazon and Goodreads.
Thank you very much.

ABOUT THE AUTHOR

Katrina is an author of several Young Adult and Preteen/Middle Grade novels. Each of her released books reaching the top 100 in certain categories on the Amazon's Best Sellers Rank – a few even as high as number one.

She resides in Queensland, Australia. Her three teenage boys and husband for over nineteen years treat her like a princess. Unfortunately though, this princess still has to do domestic chores.

From a very young age, she has been a very creative person and has spent many years travelling the world and observing many different personalities and cultures. Her favourite personalities have been the strange ones, yet the ones under the radar also hold a place in her heart.

During her last extensive travels, she spent 16 nights in a bomb shelter on a Kibbutz 8 kilometers off the Lebanese border. It was to avoid Katyusha bombs that the resident volunteers decided to name her after (she is still trying to work out why).

Katrina's online home is at
www.katrinacopebooks.com

You can connect with Katrina on:

Twitter https://twitter.com/Katrina_R_Cope

Facebook
https://www.facebook.com/Author.Katrina.Cope

Instagram
https://www.instagram.com/katrina_cope_author

Pinterest
https://www.pinterest.com.au/katrinacope56

Email authorkatrinacope@gmail.com